Dick and Jane

READING COLLECTION • VOLUME 2

Something Funny

GROSSET & DUNLAP • NEW YORK

Table of Contents

Dick

Look, Dick.

Look, look.

Oh, oh.

Look, Dick.

Oh, oh.

See, Dick.

Oh, see Dick.

Sally

Look, Sally.

Look, look.

See Jane.

Oh, Jane.

See Sally.

See little Sally.

Little, little Sally.

Look, Jane.

See funny Sally.

Oh, oh, oh.

Funny little Sally.

Help, Help

Look, Dick.

See Spot.

Oh, see Spot.

Help, help.

Oh, Jane.

See Spot.

Oh, see Spot.

Come, Jane, come.

Help, help, help.

Look Dick.

See Spot and Sally.

Come see Sally.

See funny little Sally.

Sally Sees Something

Come, Sally.

Come and look.

Come and see Sally.

Funny little Sally.

Dick, Dick.

Help, help.

I see something.

Help, help, help.

I see something.

Look, Sally.

I see something.

I see Baby Sally.

Little Baby Sally.

Look, look.

See funny Baby Sally.

Something Funny

Look, Dick.

Look, look.

I see something funny.

Come and see.

Come and see Spot.

Oh, Jane.

I see something funny.

Come, Jane, come.

See Spot and Baby Sally.

Come and help.

Look Dick.

See Jane help Spot.

Oh, see something funny.

See little Spot.

Funny little Spot.

Make Something Funny

Oh, Dick, look.

I can make Tim and Puff.

Tim is yellow.

Puff is red.

Make something, Dick

Make something yellow.

Make something blue.

I can make something blue.

I can make blue cars.

I can make blue boats.

See my cars and boats.

See the funny blue boat.

See the funny blue car.

Look, Jane, look.

Up go the boats.

Up go the cars.

Up, up, go Tim and Puff.